CatKid

The Fishy Field Trip

Brian James

illustrated by
Ned Woodman

A
LITTLE APPLE
PAPERBACK

SCHOLASTIC INC.

New York Toronto London Auckland Sydney
Mexico City New Delhi Hong Kong Buenos Aires

To my faithful cat, Doggie, for all her
inspirational shenanigans!

— B.J.

No part of this publication may be reproduced, stored in a retrieval
system, or transmitted in any form or by any means, electronic, mechanical,
photocopying, recording, or otherwise, without written permission of the
publisher. For information regarding permission, write to Scholastic Inc.,
Attention: Permissions Department, 557 Broadway, New York, NY 10012.

ISBN-13: 978-0-439-88855-4
ISBN-10: 0-439-88855-7

Text copyright © 2007 by Brian James. All rights reserved. Published by
Scholastic Inc. SCHOLASTIC and associated logos are trademarks and/or
registered trademarks of Scholastic Inc.

Book design by Tim Hall

12 11 10 9 8 7 6 5 4 3 2 1   7 8 9 10 11 12/0
                                              40

Printed in the U.S.A.
First printing, August 2007

Chapter 1:

School of Fish

I, CatKid, cannot sit still.

Know why?

Because today my class is learning about oceans, that's why! And oceans are my favorite thing to learn about in school.

That's because learning about oceans means learning about fish. And it's a cat-fact that I absolutely and positively LOVE fish!

I love fish on sandwiches and fish on pizza. I even like fish on ice cream. But mostly, I like fishsticks. Those fishes on a stick are the yummiest!

And plus, Mrs. Sparrow, my teacher,

says she has a surprise for us if we are good. Mrs. Sparrow goes over to the board. She asks us if we can name any animals that live in the ocean.

I can think of a bunch!

So I raise my hand as high as I can.

Then I lick my lips just thinking about all of those fish in the ocean.

But Mrs. Sparrow doesn't call on me. She calls on Bradley instead.

"Sharks!" Bradley yells out.

Bradley is what I call a smarty-pants.

Plus, he's a show-off.

And so that means he doesn't just name one shark, he names like a thousand different kinds of sharks! "Great white sharks and hammerhead sharks and thresher sharks and megamouth sharks," he says.

Mrs. Sparrow can't even write as fast as he names them.

My hand gets tired, so I put it down and wait for Bradley to finish. Only he

never finishes!
After naming
the sharks, he
starts naming
other things
like manta
rays and eels.

"Hey, don't hog all the answers," I holler, because I, CatKid, will be very, very mad if he steals my answer.

And guess what?

It works, that's what!

Bradley doesn't name any more animals.

So I put my hand back up in the air. And I move it around, too. Then I stand up a little so that my hand will be the highest. Mrs. Sparrow will have to call on me now.

Only that boy Billy who sits behind me ruins the whole thing!

3

"Hey, CatKid hit me in the face with her tail!" he shouts. Then he gives my tail a yank.

I turn around real quick. Then I make a huff and fold my arms at him. "Yeah, only it's not my fault, so there!" (I can't help it if my tail goes all twitchy when I get excited.)

"Okay, settle down," Mrs. Sparrow says. Then she asks Billy if he can name an animal. I make a pout and frown my whiskers. That's called *waiting your turn.*

"I know, I know!" Billy says, "Whales! They're the biggest animals. They can flatten anything with their tails!"

I roll my eyes.

I think maybe a whale flattened his brain.

But then I forget all about Billy. That's because Mrs. Sparrow calls the best name next. My name!

"FISH!" I shout.

Then I smile my whiskers real wide because those fish make me happy.

"Can you be more specific?" Mrs. Sparrow asks me.

I scratch my head and think about that one for a second. "Specifically, any kind of fish you can eat!" I say and rub my tummy.

Shelly turns around and makes a face at me. She is my number one *unfriend*. That means she is NOT my friend. That's because she thinks she's better than everyone else.

"She means what are the names, Dumb Ears!" Shelly says.

I don't like it one bit when she calls me Dumb Ears. It's just not nice and really ruffles my whiskers, so I pretend I didn't even hear her. Then I name a whole bunch of fish that are good to eat. "Tuna fish, flounder fish, and crab fish. Only crabs are not even fish, but they sure are yummy!"

"Very good, CatKid," Mrs. Sparrow says and she writes all those yummy things on the board.

Soon the whole board is filled up.

I had no idea there were so many things in the ocean.

Then comes the best part. Mrs. Sparrow passes out the crayons. She says we all get to draw a picture of our favorite ocean animal.

Drawing is my best subject.

I don't know why our class doesn't do drawing all the time instead of math and spelling. If I were the teacher, I'd have drawing time for half of the day, and recess for the second half.

And plus, another best part about drawing is that we get to sit in groups. That means I get to sit with Maddie. She's super great. Plus she's my bestest friend in the whole wide world.

"I'm going to draw a porcupine fish," I tell Maddie. That's my favorite fish because it puffs up. That puffing makes me giggle. And plus its name is like me, one whole-half something and one whole-half something else. Only its name is a trick because it's not even half porcupine. Except it does have spikes, but they are not the same kind that a porcupine has.

That fish is one sneaky fish.

Then Billy comes up behind me. "You should draw a catfish," he teases. Then he makes his cheeks into a fishy face.

"Only know what? Most catfish don't live in the ocean, that's what! They like freshwater and the ocean water is all salty like soup!" I say.

"So what?" he asks.

"So, it couldn't be my favorite *ocean* animal, and Mrs. Sparrow told us to draw our favorite *ocean* animal. So there!" I say. Then I turn away from him.

"Well anyway, it doesn't matter what you draw," he says. "I'm drawing a killer whale and they beat anything you draw!"

I wish I had spikes like a porcupine fish. Then I'd give that Billy the Bully a sneaky surprise.

But just then, Mrs. Sparrow tells us her own sneaky surprise.

"Class, I have an announcement," she says. "Next week, we're going on a field trip to the aquarium."

The whole class cheers.

I, CatKid, am so excited that I don't even know what to do with myself! I've always wanted to go to an aquarium, but I've never been allowed. My mom and dad always thought I'd be too wild around so many fish.

Only now, they have to let me go because the whole class is going, and that's what my mom calls *educational*.

My eyes go real big, and I clap my hands together. This fishy field trip is going to be the best field trip ever!

Chapter 2:

Permission Granted

I gulp really hard. Mrs. Sparrow just told us that there is only one day left for us to turn in our permission slips. I, Catkid, have a very big, serious problem. That's because I haven't even told my mom or dad about the aquarium business yet.

That's because I can't find a good time to ask them — not a single one! I was going to ask them yesterday after dinner. Only my mom made surprise cookies and that made me forget. That eating cookies stuff is what my dad calls *being distracted*.

And plus, I was going to ask them the day before that but I didn't. Only that

time it wasn't my fault. It was the bathtub's fault. That's because it spilled water all over the floor when I was pretending to be a submarine during bathtime. That put my mom in a grumpy mood. It's never a good idea to ask for something important when parents are in a grumpy mood. And asking them to sign my permission slip is super important.

Mrs. Sparrow says any kid who doesn't have a signed permission slip can't go on the field trip.

That would be the worst thing ever!

I'd have to spend the whole day in the other second-grade classroom while my class was having fun at the aquarium. And I wouldn't get to see any fish.

So no matter what, I have to ask my parents tonight because I, CatKid, have zero signed permission slips. And it's not really the tub's fault, or my mom's cookies. The secret truth is, I'm a teeny tiny bit afraid to ask. They could say no, and then I don't even know what I'd do.

When the bell rings, Maddie runs up to me. "Did you ask your mom and dad yet?" she asks me as we get on our bus.

"No way!" I say. I almost tell her about the bathtub but then I stop. That's because overflowing bathtubs are funny business and this is serious.

"Why not?" Maddie asks.

I look at Maddie and scrunch up my nose. Then I look around to make sure no one is listening. "Because every time

I'm about to ask them, my stomach goes funny," I whisper to her. "That's the secret truth."

"Why does it make your stomach funny?" Maddie whispers back.

"You know their rule about me and aquariums. They think I'll run all crazy around that place," I tell her. "It would be the worst thing ever if they say no."

"Oh," Maddie says. Then she puts her finger up to her chin. That means she's thinking. "You need a plan to make sure they say yes," she says.

Then I smile my whiskers because that plan stuff is good stuff. So I start thinking right away. But I can't think of anything. "Only one problem," I say. "What is my plan?"

Maddie scratches her

head and does some thinking, too. Finally, she puts her finger up in the air. That means she's thought of something.

"I know!" she shouts. "Whenever I want something, I always promise my mom that I won't tease my baby brother."

I squint my eyes and wrinkle my nose. That's the face I make to tell Maddie her brain is being silly. "Yeah, but I don't even have a baby brother," I tell her.

"Yeah, but you could make a different kind of promise," Maddie says. Then I smile again because that's a good plan. Maddie sure is one smart cookie.

"I'll give it a try," I say.

When the bus stops at my house, Maddie wishes me good luck. Then she gives me the thumbs-up from the window as I race to my door.

My mom and dad are both at home. I throw off my shoes and pull the permission slip out of my backpack. Then I run into the kitchen where they are. Now comes the tricky part. Because I still haven't come up with a promise.

"Hey, there," my dad says.

"Hey, there, right back!" I say.

"What's that?" he asks.

I look at my hand and see the permission slip. My mouth drops open to make a YIKES! I didn't want them to see that before I had my plan all figured out.

I quickly hide it behind my back.

"Um . . . nothing," I say.

But know what?

My dad always knows when I'm fibbing, that's what. So he comes over and takes the permission slip out of my hand. My stomach starts going all funny as he reads it. Then he shows it to my mom.

My mom looks at my dad and he looks back at her. Then they make weird faces at each other and start shrugging their shoulders. That's how parents talk to each

other when they don't want kids to know what they're saying.

Somehow I have to get them to say yes.

"Here's the thing," I say. "My whole entire class is going to the aquarium. That means it's educational. So you have to sign that permission slip for me, please. Thank you."

My mom makes a face.

"I don't know," she says.

I make my eyes go sad and my ears go droopy. Every kid knows *I don't know* is the same thing as plain old N-O.

Time for Plan B!

Plan B is Maddie's plan. It means I have to make a promise. What should I promise? What would they really, really want?

"Please! Please! Pretty please with sugar and sardines on top?" I ask. "If you let me go, I promise I'll be on my bestest cat behavior."

Then I say please a whole bunch more times.

I've just got to see that aquarium place!

"Well," my dad says, "you are in second grade."

"Yeah that's right," I say, "I'm not even a kitten anymore. I'm a full-grown CatKid!"

Then I smile real proud.

That even makes my mom smile.

Then they give each other more funny looks.

"Do you promise to follow ALL of the aquarium rules?" she asks.

I jump up and down. "I promise! I promise!"

And that's when they take the permission slip from me and sign their names.

"YIPPIE SKIPPY!" I shout and clap my hands. "Thank you! Thank you! You're the best!"

Then I do my happy dance in the hallway. I jump around on one leg, hold my tail with both hands, and spin around in circles like an ice skater.

"But," my dad says 'cause I'm still doing my happy dance, "we'll have to go over some family rules of our own."

I stop that dance right away.

Then I make my face serious.

"Sure thing," I say. I'll follow any rules they want as long as they let me go.

Chapter 3:

Ready, Set, Rules!

The night before the field trip, I make a list of everything I will need.

Then I go over it to make sure I'm not forgetting anything.

Fishing pole?

Check.

Tackle box!

Check.

Fishing hat?

Check.

Then I laugh because that fishing hat is shaped like a fish. It's my favorite hat. I got it for my last birthday. I wear it on every fishing trip. That's because it's lucky. Plus, it always cracks me up.

I look back at my list.

Permission slip?

I rush over to my bed and grab that signed permission slip out from under my pillow. I keep all of my important stuff under there. It's right next to my Christmas list for next year and a spare letter for the Tooth Fairy. I keep that just

in case a tooth falls out in my sleep. I wouldn't want to miss getting my money.

I put the permission slip with the rest of my stuff.

"That's everything," I say. I have all the things I'll need for a super special fishing trip at the aquarium. And I, CatKid, love fishing! The last time I went with my dad, I stuck my paw right in the water and swatted at the fish. I splished and splashed those fish all over the place.

Thinking about that splishing and splashing cracks my head up. I'm still laughing about it when I hear a *knock*! on my bedroom door.

"Who is it?" I ask.

"Your dad," my dad says.

"What's the secret password?" I ask.

"Open the door or I'll tickle you," my

dad says. That's not the password, but I open the door anyway. Then I giggle because my dad NEVER remembers the password.

My dad says we need to go over the extra rules for the field trip. I sit my tail down on my bed. I rest my chin down on my hand and perk up my ears.

"Okay, I'm ready," I say.

Only my dad doesn't even say anything. He just keeps staring at my fishing stuff.

Then he scratches his head just like I do when I'm thinking.

"Um, kitten?" he asks, "What's all this for?"

"For fishing! What else?" I say. Then I giggle because sometimes my dad is so silly that I don't even mind that he called me kitten.

He sits down next to me on my bed and clears his throat. He only does that when there's something important to tell me.

"Sweetie, an aquarium isn't for fishing," he says.

I squint my eyes and give him a long look. "Are you trying to trick me?" I ask. Sometimes my dad can be really tricky.

Once he tricked me into taking medicine by hiding it in an ice-cream sundae. I ate it so fast that I didn't notice.

"Nope," he says. "There's no fishing allowed."

"But that doesn't make any sense!" I say. "Why else would they have all those fish?"

"To look at," he says.

Why would anyone want to look at fish when they could be catching fish instead?

My dad says that looking at fish can be fun, too. He says I'll get to see dolphins, and swordfish, and that they even have a baby whale.

My dad says I have to leave my fishing stuff at home. I make a face, but I promised to follow the rules.

"Can I at least wear my fish hat?" I ask.

"Sure," he says.

Then he goes over the rest of the rules. No tapping on the glass, no dipping my hand into the water, and no trying to scare the fish.

There are so many rules that I don't feel like doing my happy dance anymore.

I climb into bed.

My dad gives me a kiss goodnight.

"Good night, kitten," he says.

"Good night," I mumble.

I'm beginning to think this aquarium trip isn't all it's cracked up to be.

Chapter 4:

The Wheels on the Bus

I, CatKid, am the first in line when my class gets ready to climb on the bus waiting to take us to the aquarium.

And I'm so excited to ride on the bus that I forget all about the stinky NO FISHING part of the trip. Because a bouncy bus ride is almost the best part of a field trip. It's like the flashing space ride at the amusement park, only not as fast and dizzy.

"All aboard!" I shout when the bus driver swings the door open.

Then I rush to the seats all the way in

the back. Those seats are the coolest. And I, CatKid, am one cool cat!

"Maddie!" I shout when I see her get on the bus. Then I wave my hands around. "Back here, I saved you a spot next to me."

"WOW!" Maddie says, "I never sat in the backseat before."

I smile.

She sure is lucky to have a friend like me.

Preston sits in the other backseat. And that's just fine with me because Preston is my friend, even if he is a boy.

"Hey, CatKid," he says.

"Hey, right back," I say.

But then the whole backseat thing is almost ruined because Shelly sits down next to him.

"Oh, gross! I didn't know cats were allowed on the bus," she says.

"I didn't know meanies were," Maddie says. Then I give her the thumbs-up. That meanies stuff is good stuff.

Then Shelly makes a face at me. "THAT is the ugliest hat I've ever seen," she says.

Then Maddie takes a long look at my hat, too.

So does Preston.

I try to look up at my hat, but I can't see it on the top of my head.

"I don't think it's ugly," Maddie says, "I think it's fish-tastic!"

"Me, too," Preston says.

"Yeah, me three," I say.

That makes three against one. That

means Shelly loses. Mrs. Sparrow taught us that. She calls it *voting*.

Shelly rolls her eyes.

She looks like she wants to say something, but nothing comes out of her mouth. She just stays quiet and turns her head away. That's what my mom calls *the cat getting her tongue.*

Just then, the bus pulls out of the school parking lot. Now my stomach is full of excitement because we are on our way.

The bus bounces up and down and down and up as I watch our school shrink away behind us.

Then my stomach starts to feel a little funny. Whenever I get carsick, my mom tells me to think of something else. Sometimes we play games to take my mind off of feeling yucky.

Only I can't think of anything, so I ask Maddie to come up with a game.

"I know," she says. "Let's sing a song."

"Good idea," I say. Nothing is more fun on a bus trip than singing songs.

"What should we sing?" I ask.

"Let's make up a song," she says.

"Double good idea!" I say, and already I don't feel carsick anymore.

Then we start to sing "The Wheels on the Bus." Only we make up our own words. We make up ocean words.

"The waves in the sea go splish and
    splash,
    Splish and splash,
    Splish and splash.
The waves in the sea go splish and
    splash,
    all through the day."

Then we sing it again. And again. And one more time, too. I love to sing! All cats love to sing even if they're not too good at it.

We are just about to sing the second part about sharks in the sea going bite and chomp when Shelly stops us.

"THAT'S NOT SINGING!" she shouts. "THAT'S HOWLING!"

"Only know what?" I say. "You're not the boss of the bus, that's what!" Besides, I can't help it if I howl. That's how cats sing.

So, me and Maddie start to sing again.

Shelly covers her ears and starts singing her own song about the cat on the bus going hiss and howl. I don't even mind one bit, because that hiss and howl song is one clever song.

I'm about to sing that song, too, when Mrs. Sparrow asks all of us for our attention. So I quiet my mouth and listen.

Those are the rules, and I, CatKid, promised to follow all of the rules.

Mrs. Sparrow is holding a bunch of papers in her hand. She says we're going on a fish fact-finding mission. Then she hands the papers to Bradley in the front seat. She tells him to take one and pass the rest back.

"What is it?" our whole class asks.

"It's a treasure hunt," she says.

A treasure hunt!

That's the best news I've heard all day.

I take a peek at that paper when it finally gets all the way back to me. It's a whole list of fish riddles. Then I smile my whiskers. I, CatKid, love riddles, especially ones about fish!

Maddie reads the first one. "This animal isn't a fish at all. It comes to the surface of the water to breathe." There is a space next to it for the answer. There are also lots of riddles. There are three questions after each riddle. The questions are these:

1. *Where do these animals live?*
2. *What do they eat?*
3. *Who are their enemies?*

"It looks like one tough treasure hunt," I whisper to Maddie and she nods.

Mrs. Sparrow says that we need to look and listen as our class goes through the aquarium. "Try to fill in as many answers as you can. The person sitting next to you will be your teammate."

I look at Maddie.

Maddie looks at me.

That's what I call a good team.

Then I look at Preston.

Poor Preston has to have Shelly on his team.

That's what I call a stinky team.

"The team that answers the most questions correctly will win a special prize!" Mrs. Sparrow says.

The whole bus makes *oooohhhhs* and *aaahhhhhs* because everybody likes special prizes.

Mrs. Sparrow gives the best special prizes in the whole second grade. Some teachers only give normal stickers and pencils. Mrs. Sparrow gives *glow-in-the-dark* stickers and *glitter* pencils!

Me and Maddie LOVE *glow-in-the-dark* stickers and *glitter* pencils!

"Do you think we can win?" she asks me.

I take a look at the questions.

"You bet!" I say. Then I smile real big. "I'm very good at treasure hunts. I can sniff out the answers with my cat senses!"

If there wasn't a rule on the bus about staying in your seat, I would do my happy dance. That's because I, CatKid, am very happy.

Fish, treasure hunts, and now special prizes!

I can't even wait to get to this place.

Chapter 5:

City of Fish

The bus comes to a stop in front of the aquarium. I press my face against the window and stare my eyes real wide at it.

It's GINORMOUS!

It is bigger than the mall, and I thought the mall was the biggest building in the whole world.

And plus, the aquarium is all silver and shiny. It sparkles even more than Mrs. Sparrow's *glitter* pencils.

I just can't stop staring at that aquarium place. "Can you believe how big that place is?" I ask Maddie.

She takes a peek and shakes her head.

"There must be a whole city of fish in there!" I say.

"Well, let's go see," Maddie says. Before we go, I take off my fish hat and put it on my seat. Mrs. Sparrow says I'm not allowed to wear it inside. That's a rule! Plus, it might scare those fishes. So my lucky hat is going to have to stay here and save my seat until I get back.

Maddie takes my hand and pulls me right off the bus where the rest of our

class is waiting to go inside the aquarium.

As soon as we step through the door, we are in a long tunnel. The walls of the tunnel are made of glass. Even the ceiling is made of glass. And the other side of the glass is filled with water.

It's like walking on the bottom of the ocean.

I don't even know where to turn my tail!

I've never seen so much water all over the place. There's more water than at the town swimming pool. I bet they could fit a gazillion of those pools in here. And I don't mean the little pool where all babies swim, I mean the big grown-up pool!

And know what else?

THERE ARE FISH IN THAT WATER!

They are everywhere.

Fish on this side of me.

Fish on that side of me.

And even fish above my head!

"Psst, CatKid," Maddie whispers, "you're drooling."

I stop staring at the fish and wipe my mouth with my sleeve. Then I look around to make sure no one else saw.

The coast is clear.

"Thanks," I say. Then I wipe my forehead, because that was a close one. I wouldn't want anyone to see because second graders are NOT supposed to drool. That's baby stuff.

But I can't help it. Watching all these fish makes my stomach grumble.

Mrs. Sparrow tells us to form a straight line. "Make sure you stand next to your teammate," she reminds us.

Only know what?

I can't stand still, that's what!

I want to chase those fish all over the place and show them who's boss cat around here. I know I promised that I wouldn't, but I *really* want to take off.

Maddie grabs hold of my tail. Then she reaches into her backpack and takes out a cookie. "I thought this might happen," she says, "so I brought some cookies in case you got frisky."

My nose goes all sniffy when I smell the cookie, so I forget all about those fish for a second. And eating that cookie makes my stomach stop grumbling, too.

"Thanks, I needed that," I say.

That Maddie sure is a cat's best friend!

Just then, Mrs. Sparrow introduces us to a man who works at the aquarium. "This is our tour guide, Mr. Fisher."

That makes my whole class giggly. That's because that Fisher name is a funny name for someone who works at an aquarium.

"Hello, kids," Mr. Fisher says.

"Hello!" we say right back. That's called being polite.

First, Mr. Fisher goes over the rules. I pay attention to those rules. I don't want to break them by accident. My mom and dad would not be happy.

After that, Mr. Fisher leads us into the main part of the aquarium. In the first big room, the walls are even taller than my house! It is dark in the room, but behind the glass it's all sunshiny under the water. There sure is a lot of water! AND A LOT OF FISH!

There are all different kinds of fish, too. Striped fish and rainbow fish. Big

fish and tiny fish. Funny round fish and skinny fish. But the one thing they all have in common is that they are all what I call YUMMY!

Kendra, my second best friend, turns around.

"Isn't this great?" she asks. "Look at all of the amazing fish!"

"I'm trying not to," I say.

"How come?" she asks.

"Because all of these fish are making me hungry," I say. I don't know if I can even make it all the way to lunchtime. Lucky for me, Maddie sneaks me another cookie.

Chapter 6:

Underwater Planet

Maddie holds on to my tail as we start the tour. I asked her to. That way I won't run off to chase after those fish. That would break more than one rule. It would break the *no chasing fish* rule and the *no wandering off* rule. And I almost forgot the *no running* rule. Breaking those rules would put me in hot water, so I stay close to Maddie.

For the first stop on the tour, our class walks through another tunnel. This tunnel is dark. Some of the kids in my class make spooky noises. But it's not spooky to me, because my cat eyes can see in the dark.

"This is like being on a submarine," Preston whispers.

"Exactly like being on a submarine," I tell him.

"How do you know? You've never been on a submarine," Shelly says.

"Yeah, only know what? I've seen it on TV and that's almost the same thing, so there!" I say to her.

Shelly is just about to say something back at me when her mouth drops open. Then my mouth drops open, too. That's because we step into a new room that is absolutely, positively like a submarine!

It's a giant circle, with windows all around. And just like on a submarine, we're underwater. Not really, but the fish tanks make it feel like we're underwater. Plus those tanks are lit up, so the water sparkles like stars.

I rush up to the glass and take a long look. Those tanks are swarming with jellyfish as big as my head! They look like gooey blobby balloons and they wobble when they swim. Also, they have super long tentacle thingies that dangle everywhere like string.

Mr. Fisher tells us that the jellyfish in this tank are lion's mane jellyfish. "They are one of the deadliest kinds in the world," he says. And for the first time, I sure am glad that the glass is there. I wouldn't even want to touch those stingy fish.

"Psst! CatKid," Maddie whispers. "I think jellyfish are the answer to this riddle."

She points to one of the clues. *This fish sounds good with peanut butter, but you wouldn't want to eat it.*

"You're right!" I whisper back. So we write our answer next to that clue. Then we listen to Mr. Fisher. We still have the three questions, about what jellyfish

eat, where they live, and who are their enemies. If we listen, Mr. Fisher just might give us the answers!

He tells us that some animals, like sea turtles, don't mind getting stung by jelly-fish. That's because the jellyfish's stingy stuff doesn't bother them. "Some sea turtles eat jellyfish," Mr. Fisher says.

I think about eating jellyfish. It makes me grab my tummy and stick out my tongue. Then I make a face like feeling sickish. "Yuck!" I say.

I want to forget all about eating jellyfish,

but then Maddie points to the treasure hunt questions. One of them asks about their enemies. That means what animals eat them. And one of those answers is sea turtles. That's what Mrs. Sparrow meant about listening. And lucky for me, my cat ears have very, very good hearing.

Then Mr. Fisher tells us that jellyfish like to live in cold water. He says they eat small fish. Those are both answers, so we write them down.

After the jellyfish room, Mr. Fisher says he's taking our class to a very special room. But it doesn't seem very special to me. There aren't any glass walls or funny spaceship lights.

When I tell that to Kendra, she points to these big round things that look like swimming pools. "Don't you know what those are?" she asks.

I shake my head.

"Those are touch tanks!" she says. "We get to hold starfish *for real*!"

My ears perk right up.

"And it's not against the rules?" I ask. I have to make sure.

"Nope," Kendra says with a big smile.

I clap my hands and hurry over to one of the petting pools. Mr. Fisher asks me if I'd like to hold a sea star.

"Yes, please!" I shout.

"Don't let her do it, she'll eat it," I hear Billy say.

I make a growly face at him. "That's not true," I say. "I love stars! All kinds! I love the ones that live in the sky and even the ones that live in the sea!"

I tell Mr. Fisher all about how I make wishes on stars sometimes. "Once, I wished for a pony. Only I didn't get it," I tell him. "My mom says it's because there are no ponies in space, and that's where the wishes come from."

Mr. Fisher smiles. And then guess what? He lets me have a turn putting my hand in the touch tank, that's what!

And guess what else?

I reach down in the water and pick up a starfish with my hand! It has five pointy arms and feels like a squishy rock. Plus

it's so tickly that it makes me shout a little bit.

"Don't worry, they won't bite. They only feed on teeny tiny animals that are so small you can't see them," Mr. Fisher tells me.

I look over at Maddie and she looks at me. That's another answer on the treasure hunt. We'll have to try to remember that, because right now we're too busy petting all those little swimming stars.

Chapter 7:

Showtime

The next place we go is the aquarium theater. There's a giant swimming pool in the center and seats all around it.

Mrs. Sparrow shows us where to sit. And guess what? We get to sit in the front row, that's what!

"I hope it's a shark show," I hear Billy say.

"I hope it isn't," I say. I don't like sharks. They're bullies! Just like Billy.

"It can't be a shark show," Maddie tells him. "Nobody would go swimming with sharks." Then she points to the people swimming in the pool.

I wonder if Mr. Fisher knows about that. I'm pretty sure it's against the rules to swim in the pool. So I raise my hand and wave him over.

"Are they allowed to swim in there?" I ask him.

Mr. Fisher pats me on my cat head. "Sure." he says. "they are the people who work with the dolphins."

Shelly turns her head right around.

"DOLPHINS?" she shouts. "Are we going to see a dolphin show?"

Mr. Fisher nods his head.

Shelly can't even believe her ears. Neither can I. I've never seen a dolphin show before. And dolphins are what I call really cool. Also, dolphins don't make me hungry because they are not even fish. They're mammals. So are whales. That means they can't breathe underwater and have to come up for air. Mrs. Sparrow taught us that last week.

In fact, I think that's the answer to one of the riddles. I whisper it to Maddie. "I have a beak, but I'm not a bird. I swim, but I'm not a fish."

"That's it," Maddie says. "Dolphins have long noses called beaks, and they aren't fishes!" So we write that dolphin answer down.

When it's time for the show to start, I clap my hands. Then two dolphins swim across the pool. Only they don't swim like normal. They swim standing up, with only their tails in the water!

But that swimming isn't even the most amazing part. Next, the dolphins dive through hoops. Then they dive back underwater and make a big splash.

I clap my hands because that is one good trick. I think I'm getting the hang of this aquarium thing. I could sit and watch these dolphins swim all day long.

Then, the trainer gets out of the pool.

"Is the show over?" I ask Maddie.

"No, now he's going to feed the dolphins," Maddie whispers back.

"Oh," I say. "That sounds like fun."

Only know what?

It's zero fun, that's what.

That's because when the trainer guy holds up the dolphin food, I see it's a fish. I can sniff it all the way from my seat.

I want to jump right up and rush right down there. But Maddie is already holding on to my tail to keep me from breaking the rules.

I lick my lips. Watching those dolphins eat makes me really, super hungry. And to make it worse, those greedy dolphins eat every fish in the bucket. If I was allowed down there, I would tell those dolphins a thing or two about sharing.

By the time the show is over, not even more cookies could make me stop thinking about fish. Lunch cannot come soon enough!

Chapter 8:

Brainy Fish

After the show, Mr. Fisher takes us all over the place. I get dizzy going to so many rooms and walking through so many tunnels. And plus, after watching those dolphins pig out, I can't stop staring at all the fish and thinking about how yummy they might taste.

I watch a huge octopus swimming right in front of my eyes.

I have to keep wiping my breath off the glass so I can see. And I almost tap on it because that octopus keeps staring at me. But then I remember what my dad said about not tapping. So I don't, because a

promise is a promise. And a rule is a rule.

But I can't stop thinking about getting my paws on that octopus. It would make one GIANT octopus pizza!

Octopus is not even one of my favorite foods. In fact, most of the time I think they are gross. But my stomach starts going *rumble* and *grumble* so loud that I'm starting to think it would be yummy.

I'm so busy thinking about it that my cat ears don't notice Maddie behind me. So I'm not even ready for it when she taps me on the shoulder.

I leap straight up in the air!

When I land on my feet, my tail is all bushy. That always happens when I'm not ready for something like being tapped on the shoulder.

Maddie covers her mouth and laughs.

"Your tail is a little bit like a puffer fish," she giggles. Then she puffs her cheeks and I laugh, too. She's right. My tail does look funny all puffed up.

Then Maddie stops smiling. She wrinkles up her nose and looks at the treasure hunt paper. That means she is getting down to business.

"I think the answer to this riddle is the octopus," she says.

I look at the riddle. *This animal's long arms can wave hello and good-bye to four people at the same time.* I do the math in my head. To wave hello and good-bye takes two hands. It would take eight hands to wave to four people, just like an octopus has eight tentacles.

"Hey, that's right," I say. Then I make a fist and squint my eyes. That is my smarty face. "What are the other octopus questions?" I ask.

Maddie smiles. "It's still the same questions as for all the other animals." Then she calls me a silly kitty. And I don't mind because silly kitty is a good thing to be called. My dad calls that a pet name.

Then Maddie reads the questions again.

1. *Where do they live?*
2. *What do they eat?*
3. *Who are their enemies?*

"Oh, yeah," I say. "Those sure are hard questions."

Maddie nods her head.

"How about we make up the answers," I say. "That would be funny."

Then I think of good made-up answers.

"They live in this aquarium. They like

to eat pizza. And their enemies are me, CatKid, because I would like to dive right into that tank."

"You'll never win with those answers!"

I turn around and see Bradley standing right behind me.

"Yeah, never," Billy says.

Billy is his teammate.

And I take back that part about Preston and Shelly being a stinky team. They are only half stinky. Billy and Bradley are one hundred percent the stinkiest team EVER!

"That shows what you know," I say, "because I was only joking."

"Doesn't matter," Bradley says, "because I know more facts than anyone, so we are going to win the prize."

I make a huff.

That Bradley really gets on my cat nerves when he thinks he knows everything! And Billy gets on my cat nerves because he's not even doing any of the work.

I'm just about to give them a piece of my mind when Mrs. Sparrow tells us to line up. "We're going to head up to the cafeteria," she says.

And besides the special prize business, that is the second best news I've heard all day because I, CatKid, am STARVING!

I turn and make a face at Bradley the Know-It-All. "Let's go," I say to Maddie. "My stomach is telling me that it's time for lunch."

Chapter 9:

Where Are the Fishsticks?

The cafeteria at the aquarium is not like the cafeteria in our school. Our cafeteria is also the gym. So sometimes it smells like old socks. Plus, you don't have to take an elevator to our cafeteria because it is on the same floor as the rest of our school.

But not at the aquarium. The whole entire roof of this cafeteria is made of glass, so it looks like the ceiling is the sky.

"This lunchroom is like a castle!" Kendra says.

"Yeah, a sand castle," I say, "only with-out the sand."

And the best part of all is that I get to buy lunch.

Buying lunch is a special treat.

I never get to buy lunch at school. My dad always packs my lunch. I reach into my pocket for the money my dad gave me.

Ten whole dollars!

Part of it is supposed to be for buying something at the gift shop. Only I might spend it all on food because I, CatKid, have never been so hungry in my whole life.

Once we are in line, I take a peek at the menu.

They have chicken and cheeseburgers, hot dogs and salads, but I don't see any fishes on a stick.

I check again. I read it from top to bot-tom and side to side.

And guess what?

Absolutely NO fishes on a stick, that's what!

No fish at all.

This place makes no sense. There are fish swimming all over, in every room, but not in the one room where they really should be.

When it is my turn to order, I make a frown. The lady behind the counter asks me what I want.

"Do you have any fish? Any fish at all?" I ask.

"No, I'm sorry," she says.

TODAYS LUNCH
HOT DOGS
HAMBURG
PIZZA
SOUP

SUE

TER

I knew those dolphins ate them all!

"I guess I'll have a hot dog then, please. Thank you," I say. But I don't even mean the thank-you part. I only said that part to be nice.

I pay for my hot dog and sit down next to Maddie.

"That looks delicious," Maddie says. Maddie's mom packed her a lunch. It's a boring cheese sandwich.

Maddie looks at my hot dog again. Then she rubs her tummy because Maddie likes hot dogs almost as much as I like fishes on a stick. "Can I have a bite?" she asks.

"Sure thing," I say.

I trade her a bite of my hot dog for two more cookies. That's a fair trade.

"*Mmmmmmm, Mmmmmm!*" Maddie says and licks her lips. "That's one good hot dog."

"Yeah, I just wish it was a dogfish hot dog," I say.

"What's a dogfish?" Kendra asks.

"Is it one whole-half dog and one whole-half fish like your cat half and kid half?" Preston asks.

I shake my head.

"Nope, there's really no dog at all. It's a kind of shark. They only call them dogfish because they travel in packs like dogs do," I say. "My dad told me all about them once when we went fishing."

"Do they eat catfish?" Preston asks.

"No way!" I say. "Catfish are sooo much tougher than dogfish." Then I smile real proud because cats are better than dogs, even underwater. "Besides, catfish live mostly in freshwater and dogfish like salt water. So dogfish eat other sharks, and sometimes even an octopus."

Just then, Maddie claps her hands and

points her finger in the air. "That's one of the answers," she says.

She takes out that paper and writes dogfish next to the question about enemies of the octopus. "You knew that without even looking! See, you know more about fish than that smarty-pants Bradley!"

"Hey you're right!" I say. "I do know a lot about fish." Then I smile as wide as I can.

And now that I'm not hungry anymore, I forget all about catching fish. I want to use my fish smarts to win the special prize instead. Then we'll show Bradley and Billy who is full of fish facts in our class!

I finish my hot dog in one last bite.

I can't wait to go diving for those treasure hunt answers.

Chapter 10:

Diving for Treasure

After lunch, we see a ton of different fish. And I don't think about eating one even once. I'm too busy figuring out riddles and listening for answers.

"Look!" Maddie says as we go into a new room. "A puffer fish!"

I take a closer look.

"Only know what?" I say. "That's not a puffer fish. It's a porcupine fish!"

"How can you tell? They both puff up," Maddie says.

"Because all porcupine fish have spikes and most puffer fish don't. Plus, puffer fish are smaller," I say.

PORCUPINE FISH

"That's right," Mr. Fisher says. "You sure know your fish," he adds.

That makes me happy. I know so much about fish I might even work at this aquarium one day. That would be the best job!

But then when we get to the next room, I change my mind. That's because the name above the door says Electric Eels.

I point it out to Maddie.

Maddie makes a face. It's the same face she makes at her house when her baby brother is stinky. Then her face turns greenish.

"YUCKA!" she says.

"Double YUCKA," I say. I wouldn't

want to touch one of those eels. Eels are slimy. Plus, they are gross. I don't even like to look at them. But they are part of the treasure hunt, so we have to.

When we get into the room, Billy and Bradley are already there.

TRIPLE YUCKA!

Billy is shaking his arms and legs all over like his bones are made of jelly.

"I'm an electric eel," he says. Then he grabs my tail and shakes it. "I'm going to give you a shock!"

I grab my tail back. "If you do that one more time, *I'll* give *you* a shock," I say.

"Hey, Billy, let's go stand over there," Bradley says. "I don't want the cat to steal all of my answers."

"Yeah," Billy says. "We don't want you stealing all of his answers."

"You're supposed to be a TEAM!" I say. That means they are both supposed to be finding the answers, but Bradley's doing all the work. "And anyway, we don't need your answers."

"We're going to win all on our own, so there!" Maddie says.

"There's no way you'll beat me," Bradley says. "Come on Billy, I think her dumbness is cat-tagious!"

I stick my tongue out at Bradley when he turns around. That's the best way to stick your tongue out. Because if he can't see me do it, then he can't tattle on me. And Bradley is one big tattletale!

Now we have to win this treasure hunt!

And when we do, I'm going to smile my whiskers right at him. Then he'll know he's not the only smarty-pants in the whole world.

On the way out of the eel room, Mr. Fisher tells us that the tour is over. I can't even believe the whole day has gone by!

We say good-bye to him and he says good-bye right back.

Mrs. Sparrow is waiting to collect our treasure hunt papers as we get on the bus.

When we hand in our papers, she asks

if we had fun. Maddie and I nod our heads up and down and down and up. Because this aquarium place is a blast! Even if they don't let you go fishing.

On the way back to school, Mrs. Sparrow says she'll tell us tomorrow who won the special prize.

I'm so excited that I have to sing at the tip top of my lungs the whole way back on the bus. That's called *letting it all out.* And nothing can put me in a bad mood. Not even when Shelly covers her ears and sings her cat on the bus song. In fact, that is becoming what I call my favorite song because it sure is funny.

Chapter 11:

Home Cooking

I run right into my house when I get home from school. I drop my backpack and take off my shoes. There are no shoes allowed in my house. It's a rule, like no tapping on the glass at the aquarium.

Then I head for my favorite spot in the whole house. It is right in front of the family room window. It is the sunshiniest spot. I take all my catnaps there.

Only today I'm not snoozy at all.

I want to tell my mom and dad all about the field trip. So I get my feet warmed up and then I run and make a jumping leap onto my favorite spot.

Crash!

A perfect landing.

Now I'm ready to blabber my mouth about that city of fish. My mom and dad are not going to believe all the things they have in that place.

"MOM! DAD! I'M HOME!" I shout.

Then I quick cover my mouth with my hands because I'm not supposed to shout. Only my voice came out loud all by itself because I'm so excited.

"Wow! What a bundle of energy," my dad says.

I look down at my lap.

I check all around.

I don't see a bundle of anything.

Sometimes I think maybe my dad needs to get his eyes checked. He's always see-ing things that I don't see.

"How was your class trip?" my mom asks.

"It was cat-tastic!" I say. "And you know what?"

"What?"

"I didn't break any of those rules, not even once!" I tell them. "But I did come *this close* to tapping on the glass because an octopus was staring at me," I say. Then I hold my finger and thumb real close together so they can see how close I'm talking about.

"We're very proud of you," my dad says.

Then he smiles real big. That's his proud-of-me face. And I, CatKid, like that face. Then, he scratches me behind my ears, too. That makes me lean into him and my tail goes all waggy because I sure like that scratching.

My mom says I should tell them all about the trip. So I take a deep breath. Then I start from the very beginning.

"Once upon a time," I say, because that's the best way to start any story, "my class got on the bus and me and Maddie made up songs to sing."

Then I sing my song for them.

"And guess what? Mrs. Sparrow made up a treasure hunt game!" I tell them. "I told you she was a sneaky teacher."

Then I tell them about all the different fish we saw and how my tummy was going *grumble* and *rumble* from watching those swimmy fish. "But it wasn't even just fish," I tell them.

That's when I tell them about the swimmy mammals. I tell them about the dolphins and about how they had a real live killer whale and it was all black-and-white like a wet zebra. Then I showed them how I saw it blow water out of the top of its head. "Only it wasn't all water," I said. Then I told them how Mr. Fisher said it was also air. And that means they aren't even fish because they don't breathe underwater.

"It sounds like you learned a lot," my dad says.

I nod my head up and down. "I even learned that if a starfish loses an arm, it will grow back!"

Then I tell them about the sharks. "Mr. Fisher says that sharks keep growing new teeth." It makes me shiver thinking about all those teeth.

"It sounds like a great place," my mom says.

"You bet!" I say. Then I remember one thing that wasn't so great. "Oh, and just so you know, there are NO fish in the cafeteria. The dolphins ate them all. So next time I go, I would like to pack my lunch, please. Thank you."

"I'll keep that in mind," my dad says.

"Did you finish the treasure hunt?" my mom asks.

"Yeppers!" I say.

"Who won?" my dad asks.

"That's the thing," I tell him. Then I put my arms out to my side and shrug my shoulders, "Mrs. Sparrow won't tell us until tomorrow. It's a mystery."

Just then I remember the gift shop. Mrs. Sparrow let us go there before getting back on the bus.

I make a quick trip to my backpack.

"I almost forgot," I say. Then I look in my backpack for the gift I got them. It's the best!

Bingo!

Found it!

"Here!" I say and hand the gift to my dad.

"A bumper sticker?" he asks.

"Yeah. It says HONK IF YOU LOVE FISH!" I tell him. When I'm old enough

HONK IF YOU LOVE FISH

to have a car, I'll be honking that horn all over the place!

"Thanks," my dad says. He says he'll put it on my mom's car. I think that's pretty nice of him.

"You must be hungry after all that excitement," my mom says, and I nod my head up and down. "We have a special treat tonight," she says.

A special treat!

I love special treats.

I make my nose go all sniffy to see if I can guess. I smell it right away. And so I grab my tail and spin around like an ice skater because that smell is fishes on a stick!

YUMMY! YUM! YUM!

I race for the kitchen. Even though I learned that fish can be fun to watch, they are still fun to eat. And there's nothing better than home cooking!

Chapter 12:

First Place?

The next morning, my whole class is waiting for Mrs. Sparrow to solve the treasure hunt mystery.

"I wonder who won," Kendra says.

"Me, too," Maddie says.

"Me three," I say.

"I know it's me," Bradley says. "No one is going to beat me."

"Yeah, no one!" Billy says.

I, CatKid, don't think they know what it means to be a team. Billy let Bradley do all the work. That makes him a cheater, cheater, garbage eater!

So I tell him that.

"Cheater, cheater, garbage eater!" I shout.

"Am not!"

"ARE, TOO!"

"AM NOT!"

"ARE, TOO!" I say. "You didn't do any work. You just flopped around like an eel. I saw you!"

"So? I'm still going to win, so there!" he says.

I don't get to say anything back at him, because Mrs. Sparrow stands up in front of the class. That means all of us are supposed to quiet our shouting because she has something to say.

"Class, I've finished going over the treasure hunt papers," she says. Then she says we all did a very good job and that makes everyone smile.

"Who gets the special prize?" Kendra asks.

And just then, the mystery gets more mysterious. That's because Mrs. Sparrow says there was a tie. She says we will have a game of True-or-False trivia this afternoon to see which team wins the special prize.

I cross my fingers real tight when she reads the names of those two tied teams.

And guess what?

It works, that's what!

The first team she calls is me and Maddie's team.

I give out a quiet shout.

"HOORAY FOR US!" I whisper yell.

But then the next team Mrs. Sparrow

calls makes me hold my nose and go P.U. because it is one stinky team.

It is Bradley and Billy's team.

"HOORAY FOR US!" Billy yells.

I make a grumpy face. I can't wait to play that True-or-False game and show them which team is better.

After recess, I run into my classroom and sit down my tail. Then I tap my sneakers really fast on the floor. I always do those things when I have a little bit of nervous in me.

And I'm nervous right now because the True-or-False game is going to start any second. And that Bradley is going to be hard to beat. That makes me the under-dog. And I don't like being a dog of any kind.

I try to remember everything I know about fish. But when I try to think of those fish facts, I can't remember any of them.

So I tap faster and faster.

When Mrs. Sparrow calls us up to the front of the room, my feet are still tapping. They tap so fast they race me right up to the front of the classroom.

Maddie comes up next to me. I whisper that I have a secret. Then I tell her the secret about not remembering any fish facts.

"Don't worry," Maddie says. "You listened carefully. You'll remember."

"Thanks!" I say. That Maddie sure is a good teammate. Then my foot stops tapping and I don't feel so nervous anymore.

Mrs. Sparrow says all the questions will be about the animals from the treasure hunt. She will ask one player from each team a question. If they get it right, then a player from the other team will have to get their question right, too. We keep going until one player gives the wrong answer.

"Ready?" she asks.

I hold up my finger for her to give me a second.

I take two deep breaths and make sure my feet stay still.

"Okay, ready," I say.

The first question is for Maddie.

"True or false? The puffer fish inflates so it can take bigger breaths," Mrs. Sparrow asks.

Maddie squints her eyes. That's how she looks for answers in her brain.

"Oh, I know this one," she says. "FALSE. It puffs up to scare other fish so it's harder to eat them. CatKid taught me that!"

I give her a high five.

Then she gives me her puffer fish face and it cracks up my whiskers.

The whole class gets giggly except Bradley. That's because now it's his turn, and now his sneakers are the ones going tap-tap all over the place.

"True or false? The manta ray only eats very small fish," Mrs. Sparrow asks him.

Bradley doesn't take any time to think about it. "TRUE!" he says right away. "And those small fish are called plankton."

I roll my eyes at him for being such a show-off!

The next turn is my turn.

"True or false? The giant Pacific octo-

pus likes to live in very warm water," Mrs. Sparrow asks me. I scratch my head and think about that octopus that stared at me.

I remember touching the glass to wipe away my breath. It was cold.

Then I remember what Mr. Fisher said. He said that the octopus lived *in the cooler waters* of the Pacific Ocean.

"FALSE!" I say. "It likes the water to be colder, but I don't know why. I scream my head off when the water in the shower gets cold all of a sudden when my mom turns on the sink."

Then I show Mrs. Sparrow what I mean by making my arms shivery and my teeth chattery and saying *"Brrrrrr!"*

All the kids in my class start to laugh, even Shelly. Maddie says it's because I'm one silly kitty. And that's just fine with me. I'd rather be a silly kitty than a show-off like Bradley.

Mrs. Sparrow turns to Billy.

"True or false? The killer whale was the largest fish in the aquarium," she asks.

I cover up my mouth because I know

this one, and I wouldn't want the answer to slip out. I keep my eyes on Bradley to make sure the answer doesn't slip out of him either.

Billy folds his arms and looks up in the air. He always does that when he gets called on in class and doesn't know the answer because he wasn't paying attention.

He wasn't paying attention yesterday at the aquarium either, and so when he answers, he says, "True."

"Ha! It's false," I say, "because it's not even a fish, it's a mammal!" Mr. Fisher told us that, too.

And then I jump up and down and spin around, because me and Maddie are the winners. That's because we worked as a team and Bradley and Billy didn't.

"That's right. The answer was false. Congratulations, CatKid and Maddie," Mrs. Sparrow says.

"You mean *cat*-gratulations!" I say.

Then comes the best part.

Mrs. Sparrow goes over to her desk and opens the big bottom drawer. I open my eyes real wide because it must be an extra special prize if it's in the big bottom drawer. The pencils and stickers and stuff are all in the top drawer.

When she holds up the special prize, I make a *gulp* and I can't even believe my eyes.

Know why?

Because the prize is two real live goldfish, that's why!

The whole class goes *ooooohhhhh* and *aaahhhhh* because it is the most special of special prizes in the history of second grade. It is even more special than the glow-in-the-dark T-Rex model that Preston won for the spelling bee.

I do my happy dance all over the front of the classroom. I have my very own pet! I've never had a pet before.

"But CatKid will just eat them!" Shelly cries out.

I stop right in my tracks.

I fold my arms and hold my head up real high. "I, CatKid, would never EVER eat those fish," I say. "Those fish are the CUTEST, BESTEST, MOST ADORABLE pets I've ever even owned!"

Then Mrs. Sparrow lets me hold the bag with the goldfish. I watch them swim around and around in circles.

Then I let Maddie hold them.

"But just in case," I whisper to her, "maybe you should keep those fish at your house."

"That's probably a good idea," Maddie agrees. And that's why she's the best friend a CatKid could have.